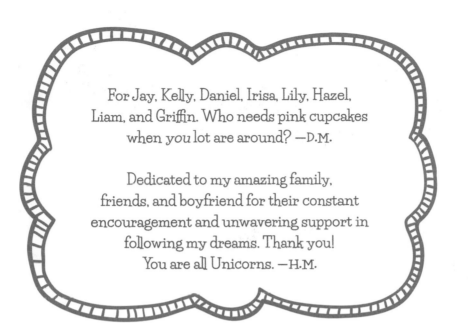

FAMILIUS

Copyright © 2018 by David Miles.
Illustration Copyright © 2018 by Hollie Mengert.

Published by Familius LLC, www.familius.com

Familius books are available at special discounts for bulk purchases, whether for sales promotions or for family or corporate use.
For more information, contact Familius Sales at 559-876-2170 or email orders@familius.com.

Library of Congress Cataloging-in-Publication Data
2017959717   pISBN 9781945547768   eISBN 9781641700269

10 9 8 7 6 5 4 3
First Edition
Printed in China

Illustration were created digitally.

UNICORN

(and Horse)

This is Unicorn.

And *THIS* is Horse.

Unicorn is a unicorn.

And Horse is, well . . .

not.

Unicorn has a sapphire horn, a silver coat,
a rainbow mane, and perfect white teeth.

Horse does not.

Unicorn eats
pink cupcakes
for every meal.

Horse does not.

Unicorn makes
rainbows.

Horse makes
something else.

Unicorn dances.
Tra la la!

Horse sits grumpy.
Blah blah blah.

Unicorn prances.
Ha ha ha!

Horse looks frumpy.
Paw paw paw.

Unicorn makes
everything cheery.

REALLY
cheery.

Horse does not.

Of course, all the
animals love Unicorn.

He has a horn for Squirrel to play ring toss.

Bird lines her
nest with his long,
beautiful hair.

And everyone loves
sharing his cupcakes.

"Won't you join us,
Horse?" said Unicorn.

NO!
I don't like you!

said Horse.

But what he meant was,

"I wish I were you."

Unfortunately, not everyone who heard about Unicorn was a happy (or unhappy) animal.

A rainbow, dancing unicorn who eats cupcakes
for breakfast could make someone a *lot* of money.

One night, while everyone was asleep, two men crept into Unicorn's paddock. Quietly as they could, they tied a startled Unicorn in ropes and loaded him into the back of their truck. Then . . .

They were off!

The other animals awoke when they heard the truck.
"Hurry! They're stealing Unicorn!"

"But I can't run fast enough to catch them!" said Squirrel.

"And I can't *fly* fast enough!" cried Bird.

"I can't run on the road!" said Fox.

"And I can't run at ALL!" said Turtle.

Only one animal could.

Horse thought.   And thought.

And thought.

Then he ran.

And ran!

And
RAN!

And with six
great chomps
of Horse's large
teeth, Unicorn
was free.

"Thank you,"
said Unicorn.

"You're welcome,"
said Horse.

This is Horse.

And this is Unicorn.

Sometimes Horse
eats cupcakes.

And sometimes
Unicorn eats hay.

Sometimes Horse
makes rainbows.

And
sometimes
Unicorn
does not.

Horse likes races.

Unicorn likes
ring toss.

But most of all, they
like each other.

Horse and Unicorn are friends.
And that's better than anything—
even pink cupcakes.